THIS CANDLEWICK BOOK BELONGS TO:

For Lawrence Birley
D.H.

To Ian with all my love
M.C.

Text copyright © 1995 by Diana Hendry
Illustrations copyright © 1995 by Margaret Chamberlain

All rights reserved.

First U.S. paperback edition 1996

The Library of Congress has cataloged the
hardcover edition as follows:

Hendry, Diana, 1941 –
Dog Donovan / by Diana Hendry ;
illustrated by Margaret Chamberlain.—1st U.S. ed.
Summary: The Donovans are afraid of so many things
that the family gets a dog from the animal shelter
to protect them.
ISBN 1-56402-537-3 (hardcover)
[1. Fear—Fiction. 2. Dogs—Fiction.] I. Chamberlain,
Margaret, ill. II. Title.
PZ7.H38586Dm   1995
[E]—dc20   94-25701
ISBN 1-56402-699-X (paperback)

2 4 6 8 10 9 7 5 3 1

Printed in Hong Kong

The pictures in this book were done
in watercolor and ink.

Candlewick Press
2067 Massachusetts Avenue
Cambridge, Massachusetts 02140

Dog Donovan

by
Diana Hendry

illustrated by
Margaret Chamberlain

CANDLEWICK PRESS
CAMBRIDGE, MASSACHUSETTS

There were seven Donovans.
They lived in a creaking,
groaning old house and
they were all scared
of something.

Old Man

Old Man Donovan
was scared of the dark.

Old Woman Donovan
was scared of spiders.

Old Woman

Dad

Dad Donovan was
scared of letters in
window envelopes.

Ma

Ma Donovan was scared of noises in the night, and there were a lot of these in the Donovan house.

Joseph James Donovan (J.J. to you) was the oldest child, and he was scared of doctors' shots.

J.J.

Molly

Molly Donovan was the middle child, and she was scared of water.

Hercules Donovan was the youngest, and he was scared of just about everything— most of all, his shadow.

Hercules

One day Ma Donovan said, "I would feel a lot less scared of noises in the night if we had a dog."

And Old Man Donovan said, "And I wouldn't be so scared of the dark."

"I suppose a dog might eat letters in window envelopes," said Dad Donovan.

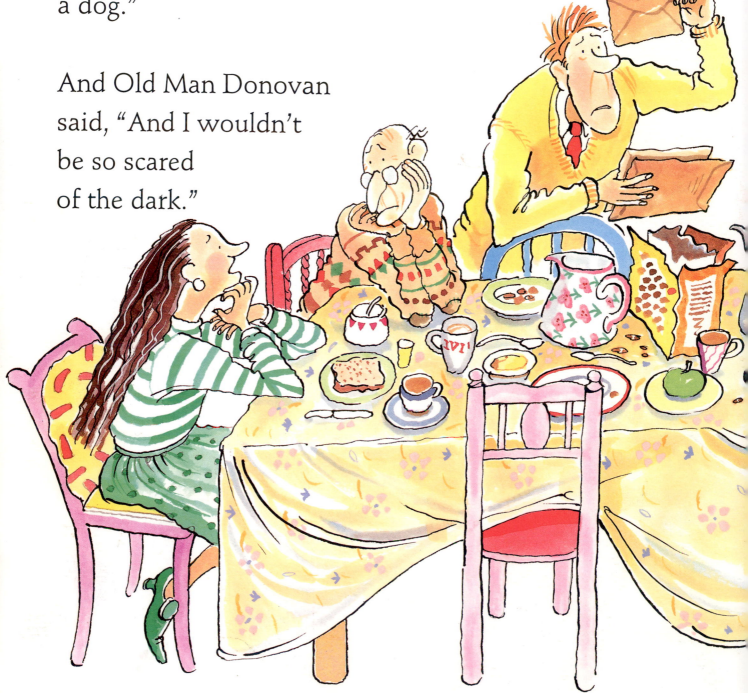

"And maybe spiders," said Old Woman Donovan.

"He could get my shots for me," said J.J.

"And doggy-paddle with me," said Molly.

"He would chase my shadow far, far away," said Hercules.

APPOINTMENT
J.J. Donovan
11:00 a.m.

So the Donovans went to the animal shelter

and bought a dog.

He was a large gray dog and his name was Hero,
so they knew immediately that he was just the
right dog for them. And he certainly was.

He was a true Donovan dog—
scared of everything.

Dog Donovan
was scared of
the mailman.

He was so scared
of the dark he had to
huddle under Old Man
Donovan's comforter.

When the wind howled
around the house and
hooted down the chimneys
and slapped shut the doors,
Dog Donovan shook
and shivered.

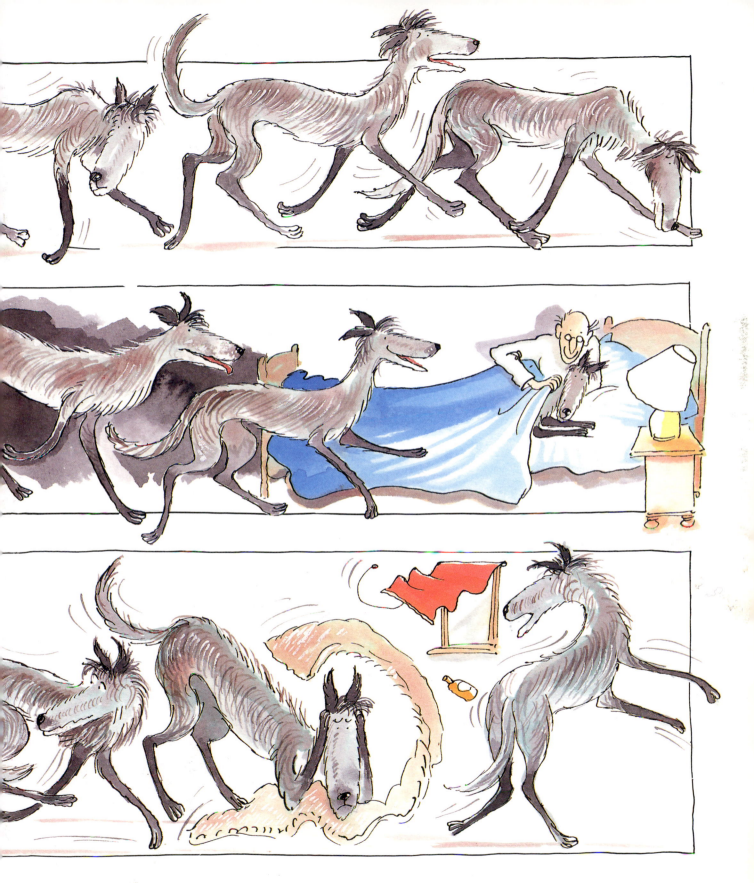

He wouldn't go near
even a puddle
of water.

When J.J. took him to the vet for his shots,
he drooped his ears
and trembled
all over.

And when he saw
his own shadow,
he chased it around and
around and around and
then hid in a dark corner
where he couldn't see it.

The spider who lived under
the stairs only had to
wave one leg
to frighten
Dog Donovan.

"There, there—you're safe with me,"
said Old Man Donovan
when Dog Donovan
huddled under his
comforter at night.

"Allow me to introduce
you to the mailman,"
said Dad Donovan.
"Then you can carry
my letters.
They won't bite."

"Noises in the night," sang Ma Donovan,
"won't make us take fright!"
And she stroked
Dog Donovan's
fur because it
was standing
on end.

"Is the big spider scaring you?" said Old Woman
Donovan, when a small spider ran past Dog
Donovan's nose and made him jump.
"I'll shoo him away."

"When the vet gives you your shot," said J.J.,
"just shut your eyes
and I'll hold
your paw."

"Let me carry you over the puddle," said Molly.

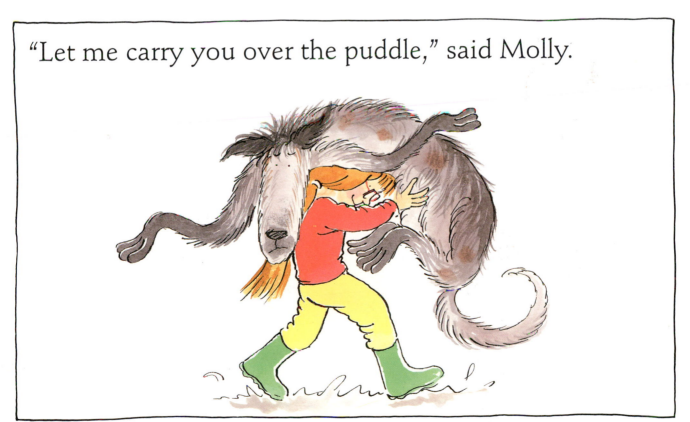

"A shadow," said Hercules, "is nothing to be scared of. Look! I can make mine dance!"

All the Donovans
felt a lot better now that they had
a dog. "We'll take care of you," J.J. told him.

"You don't need to be
scared of anything," said Molly.
"After all . . . ," said Hercules,

"you're our Hero."